Why is six afraid of seven?

Because seven ate nine.

TEACHER: 'How much is half of 8?'
PUPIL: 'Up and down or across?'
TEACHER: 'What do you mean?'
PUPIL: 'Well, up and down makes a 3 or across the middle leaves a 0.'

If there are ten cats in a boat and one jumps out, how many are left?

None; they were all copycats.

TEACHER: 'Now, class, whatever I ask, I want you all to answer at once.
How much is six plus four?'
CLASS: 'At once.'

4

LESSONS

Maths

What kind of tree does a maths teacher climb?

Geometry.

1

'If you had one pound and you asked your father for another, how many pounds would you have?'

'One pound.'

'You don't know your arithmetic.'

'You don't know my father.'

If I had seven oranges in one hand and eight oranges in the other, what would I have?

Big hands.

Why was the maths book unhappy?

It had too many problems.

What do you call a maths teacher who can make numbers disappear?

A mathemagician.

How far open were the windows in the maths class?

Just a fraction.

What did the maths teacher order for dessert?

Pi.

Why was the maths student so bad at decimals?

She couldn't get the point.

Why couldn't the seven and the ten get married?

They were under eighteen.

Why did the maths book go to the doctor?

Because it's filled with problems.

English

TEACHER: 'Do you want to hear the story about the broken pencil?'
PUPIL: 'No, thanks, I'm sure it has no point.'

TEACHER: 'What does "coincidence" mean?'
PUPIL: 'Funny, I was just going to ask you that.'

TEACHER: 'How many 'i's do you use to spell Mississippi?'
PUPIL: 'None. I can do it blindfolded.'

The teacher asked
for sentences using
the word 'beans'.
'My father grows
beans,' said a girl.
'My mother cooks
beans,' said a boy.
Then a third child spoke up,
'We're all human beans.'

TEACHER: 'If "can't" is short
for "cannot", what is
"don't" short for?'
PUPIL: 'Doughnut.'

TEACHER: 'Herman, name
two pronouns.'
PUPIL: 'Who, me?'
TEACHER: 'Correct.'

How is an English teacher like a judge?

They both hand out sentences.

What is an autobiography?

A car's life story.

Did you hear about the riot in the library?
No, what happened?
Someone found 'dynamite' in the dictionary.

'Please hush,' said the librarian to some noisy children. 'The people around you can't read.'
'Really?' asked one little girl. 'Then why are they here?'

TEACHER: 'Can you spell "caterpillar"?'
PUPIL: 'How long do I have?'
TEACHER: 'Why?'
PUPIL: 'I want to wait until he changes into a butterfly. I can spell that.'

Why did the A, E, I, O and U get in trouble?

For using vowel language.

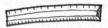

What part of English are boxers best at?

Punch-uation.

Why didn't the English student want to write poetry?

She heard that rhyme didn't pay.

What happened when the English class started writing poetry?

Things went from bad to verse.

What is the most mathematical part of speech?

The add verb.

What did the little boy use to write on when he wrote his essay about the beach?

Sandpaper.

What are the three least friendly letters?

NME.

Geography

TEACHER: 'Give me three reasons why the world is round.'
PUPIL: 'Well, my dad says so, my mum says so and you say so.'

What birds are found in Portugal?

Portu-geese.

'It's clear,' said the teacher, 'that you haven't studied your geography. What's your excuse?' 'Well, my dad says the world is changing every day. So I decided to wait until it settles down.'

TEACHER: 'Where is the English Channel?'
PUPIL: 'I don't know, my TV doesn't pick it up.'

Where do hyenas go to university?

Ha Ha vard.

TEACHER: 'Did you know that water covers two thirds of our planet?'
PUPIL: 'Certainly, that's why the ocean is always less crowded than the beach.'

What would you get if you crossed a river and a desert?

Wet and thirsty.

What is purple, has a lot of coral and lies in the ocean near Australia?

The Grape Barrier Reef.

History

'I wish I had been
born 1000 years ago.'
'Why is that?'
'Just think of all the history
that I wouldn't have to learn.'

My teacher reminds me
of history. She's always
repeating herself.

Who was the biggest
thief in history?

*Atlas. He held up
the whole world.*

'You've failed history again.'
'Well, you always told me to
let bygones be bygones.'

**Why did Henry VIII have
so many wives?**

He liked to chop and change.

What was the first thing Queen Elizabeth did on ascending to the throne?

Sat down.

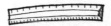

Why was the ghost of Anne Boleyn always running after the ghost of Henry VIII?

She was trying to get a head.

What is the fruitiest lesson?

History, because it's full of dates.

How was the Roman Empire cut in half?

With a pair of Caesers.

17

What was King Arthur's favourite game?

Knights and crosses.

Why did the tyrannosaurus wear a bandage?

He had a dino sore.

Teacher: 'When was
Rome built?'
Pupil: 'At night.'
Teacher: 'Why did you
say that?'
Pupil: 'Because my dad
always says that Rome
wasn't built in a day.'

Why did the Romans build straight roads?

*So their soldiers didn't go
round the bend.*

How did the Vikings tell secrets?

In Norse code.

Science

TEACHER: 'Why did the germ cross the microscope?'
PUPIL: 'To get to the other slide.'

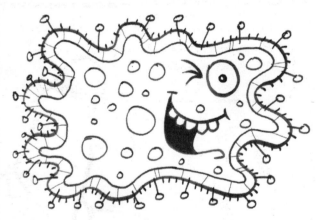

TEACHER: 'What is H20?'
PUPIL: 'Water.'
TEACHER: 'What is H204?'
PUPIL: 'To drink.'

FATHER: 'Did you finish your chemistry experiment?'
SON: 'Yes, with a bang.'

What part of your body has the best sense of humour?

Your funny bone.

**What part of your body
is the noisiest?**

Your ear drum.

**What happened when the
light broke the law?**

It went to prism.

**What petroleum doesn't have
any manners?**

Crude oil.

**What would you get if you
crossed vegetables with a
necklace?**

A food chain.

Sports

Why did the boy come first in the 100-metre sprint?

He had athlete's foot.

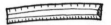

PE TEACHER: 'Why didn't you stop that ball?'
GOALIE: 'That's what the net is for, isn't it?'

What did the games teacher say to the girl who lost a hockey ball?

Find it quickly or I'll give you some stick.

What has eleven heads and runs around screaming?

A school hockey team.

What does the winner lose in a race?

His breath.

Why did Cinderella get thrown out of the rounders team?

Because she kept running away from the ball.

Why is the football pitch always wet?

Because the players are always dribbling.

25

The PE teacher was telling the class how important it was to exercise regularly. 'Look at me, for example,' he said. 'I exercise every day and I can lift three hundred pounds.'
'That's nothing, sir,' shouted a boy at the back. 'I know a woman who can lift five hundred pounds.'
'Good gracious, who's that?' gasped the teacher.
'A cashier at the bank, sir.'

The sports teacher was giving the class their very first cricket lesson.
'Now, who can tell me how to hold a bat?' he asked.
'By the wings, sir,' replied a boy.

Why were all the hurdle events cancelled?

It wasn't a leap year.

How did the football pitch end up as triangle?

Somebody took a corner.

What is the noisiest game?

Squash – because you can't play it without raising a racket.

DAUGHTER: 'Mum, can I have a new pair of plimsolls for gym, please?'
MUM: 'Why can't Jim buy his own?'

GAMES TEACHER: 'Why didn't you do the long jump?'
PUPIL: 'Because I'm short sighted, sir.'

'Are you going to watch the school football match this afternoon?'
'No, it's a waste of time. I can tell you the score before the game starts.'
'Can you? What is it then?'
'Nil nil.'

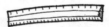

'My teacher told me to exercise with dumbbells. Will you join me in the gym?'

'What kind of marks did you get in physical education?'
'I didn't get any marks only a few bruises.'

Excuses, Excuses

PUPIL: 'Teacher, would you punish me for something I didn't do?'
TEACHER: 'Of course not.'
PUPIL: 'Good, because I didn't do my homework.'

TEACHER: 'So your dog ate your homework?'
FRED: 'Yes, teacher.'
TEACHER: 'And where is your dog right now?'
FRED: 'He's at the vet. He doesn't like maths any more than I do.'

TEACHER: 'Young man, this is the first homework assignment you've handed in all week. Why is that?'
RICHARD: 'I was in a hurry last night and didn't have time to think up a good excuse.'

I didn't do my homework because I lost my memory.
When did this start?
When did what start?

TEACHER: 'This homework looks like your mother's writing.'
PUPIL: 'Of course, I used her pen.'

SON: 'Dad, I'm tired of doing homework.'
FATHER: 'Now, son, hard work never killed anyone.'
SON: 'I know, but I don't want to be the first.'

TEACHER: 'How do you like doing your homework?'
PUPIL: 'I like doing nothing better.'

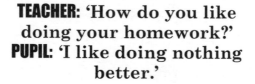

TEACHER: 'You've been ten minutes late for school every day this year and all you do is come up with stupid excuses.'
PUPIL: 'I know. If I could be fifteen minutes late that would give me enough time to come up with better excuses.'

I didn't do my homework because...

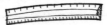

A sudden gust of wind blew it
out of my hand and I
never saw it again.

*Another pupil fell in a lake, and
I jumped in to rescue him.
Unfortunately I had to let
my homework drown.*

I used it to fill a hole in
my shoe; you wouldn't
want it now.

I made a paper plane out of it and it got hijacked.

I lost it when I was fighting this kid who said you weren't the best teacher in the school.

*ET stopped by my house
and he accidentally took it home
with him.*

**I didn't do it because I didn't
want to add to your already
heavy workload.**

Being Late

TEACHER: 'Young lady, do you know what time we start school here in the morning?'
PUPIL: 'No, teacher, I don't. I've never been here for that.'

I'm always prompt at getting out of bed in the morning. I figure the sooner I get to school, the sooner I can get back to sleep.

One kid in our class is always late for school. When we studied the Hundred Years War, he only showed up for the last three years.

TEACHER: 'Young man, you've been late for school five days this week. Does that make you happy?'
PUPIL: 'Sure does. That means it's Friday.'

Exams

TEACHER: 'I hope I didn't see you looking at Fred's test paper.'
PUPIL: 'I hope you didn't see me, either.'

TEACHER: 'You copied from
Fred's exam paper,
didn't you?'
PUPIL: 'How did you know?'
TEACHER: 'Fred's paper says "I
don't know" and you have put
"Me, neither".'

'Great news; teacher says
we have a test today
come rain or shine.'
'So what's so great
about that?'
'It's snowing outside.'

**What kinds of tests do they
give witches?**

Hex-aminations.

FATHER: 'How were the exam questions?'
SON: 'Easy.'
FATHER: 'Then why do you look so unhappy?'
SON: 'The questions didn't give me any trouble, but the answers did.'

EXAMINER: 'Never mind what the date is, get on with the exam.'
PUPIL: 'But, sir, I want to get something right.'

EXAMINER: 'You will be allowed half an hour for each question.'
PUPIL: 'How long can we have for the answer, sir?'

FATHER: 'Well, son, did you get a good place in the exams?'
SON: 'Yes, Dad, right by the radiator.'

FATHER: 'Why are your exam marks so low?'

SON: 'Because I sit at the desk at the back, Dad.'

FATHER: 'What difference does that make?'

SON: 'Well, there are so many of us in the class that when it's my turn for marks there aren't any left.'

FATHER: 'How are your exam marks, son?'

SON: 'They're underwater.'

FATHER: 'What do you mean?'

SON: 'Below C level.'

What exams does Santa Claus take?

Ho, ho, ho levels.

Why is an optician like an examiner?

They both test pupils.

What's black and white and extremely difficult?

An exam paper.

What exams do farmers take?

Hay levels.

Who got the best marks in the animal exam?

The cheetah.

EXAM QUESTION: 'What happens to gold when it is exposed to air?'
PUPIL'S ANSWER: 'It's stolen.'

EXAM QUESTION:
'Write, as precisely as possible, all you know about the great English watercolour painters of the eighteenth century.'
PUPIL'S ANSWER:
'They're all dead.'

THE TEST PRAYER
Now I lay me down to rest,
I pray to pass tomorrow's test.
If I should die before I wake,
That's one less test
I'll have to take.

FATHER: 'Aren't you first in anything at school?'
SON: 'Sure, Dad. I'm first out when the bell rings.'

TEACHER: 'Do you know why you have such poor grades?'
PUPIL: 'I can't think.'
TEACHER: 'Exactly.'

Our teacher says that he gives us tests to find out how much we know. Then all the questions are about things we don't know.

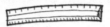

FRED: 'I bite my fingernails before easy exams.'
HARRY: 'What do you do when you're taking a hard exam?'
FRED: 'Then I bite other people's fingernails.'

FRED: 'Mum, I don't want to go to school today.'
MUM: 'Why? Have you got a stomach ache?'
FRED: 'No.'
MUM: 'Have you got a sore throat?'
FRED: 'No.'

MUM: 'Have you got
a headache?'
FRED: 'No.'
MUM: 'What have you got?'
FRED: 'A history test.'

PUPIL: 'I don't think I deserved zero on this test.'
TEACHER: 'I agree, but that's the lowest mark I could give you.'

FATHER: 'This report is terrible, Fred. It says that in your exams you came bottom in a class of twenty.'
FRED: 'It could be worse, Dad; there could be more people in the class.'

EXAMINER: 'Did you make up this poem yourself?'
PUPIL: 'Yes, sir, every word.'
EXAMINER: 'Well, pleased to meet you, William Shakespeare.'

Our teacher gives us a test every Friday. The only good thing about it is that it's followed by Saturday and Sunday.

School Trips

Where's the worst trip you're likely to go on?

To the headmaster's office.

A party of schoolchildren from the city went on a trip to the country. One of them found a pile of empty milk bottles and shouted, 'Look, miss, I've found a cow's nest.'

Did you enjoy your school trip?
Yes. We're going again tomorrow.
Why?
Search party.

A teacher took her class
on a nature trail through
the woods. She stopped by
a tree and said, 'Brian, can
you tell me what the outer
part of a tree is called?'
'I don't know, miss,'
said Brian.
'Bark, boy, bark,'
said the teacher.
'OK, miss,' said Brian.
'Woof, woof.'

Maisie went on a school trip
today. 'Our school bus had
a puncture,' she told her
mum when she returned.
'Oh dear, how did
that happen?'
'There was a fork in
the road,' Maisie told her.

TEACHER: Well, class, this year's outing will be to the seaside.

CLASS: Hooray.

TEACHER: It will cost fifty pounds . . .

CLASS: Boo.

TEACHER: . . . by train, or two pounds by coach.

CLASS: Hooray.

TEACHER: The headmaster will be coming . . .

CLASS: Boo.

TEACHER: . . . to see us off.

CLASS: Hooray.

TEACHER: The weather will be wet and windy . . .

CLASS: Boo.

TEACHER: . . . in China and warm and sunny in England.

CLASS: Hooray.

TEACHER: There will be no paddling . . .

CLASS: Boo.

TEACHER: . . . until we get there.

CLASS: Hooray.

TEACHER: Lunch will be boiled fish and cabbage . . .

CLASS: Boo.

TEACHER: . . . for me, and crisps, Coke and chocolate for you.

CLASS: Hooray.

TEACHER: There will be a visit to the museum . . .

CLASS: Boo.

TEACHER: . . . or, if preferred, to the funfair.

CLASS: Hooray.

TEACHER: But we must be back by twelve o'clock . . .

CLASS: Boo.

TEACHER: . . . midnight.

CLASS: Hooray.

'Now, children,' said the teacher as the school party was about to board the Channel ferry. 'What do we say if one of the

54

pupils falls into the sea?'
Up went Fred's hand. 'Pupil overboard, sir.'
'Very good,' said the teacher. 'And what do we say if one of the teachers falls into the sea?'
'It depends on which teacher it is, sir.'

DAD: 'How did you enjoy your school trip to the seaside, son?'
FRED: 'OK, Dad, but a crab bit my toe.'
DAD: 'Which one?'
FRED: 'Dunno. All crabs look alike to me.'

Summer
Holidays

We had huge mosquitoes on
our summer holiday. I've seen
big mosquitoes before,
but these had their own
landing strip.

I wonder if when mosquitoes go on holiday they complain about all the people?

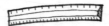

On our holiday this summer, I saw fireflies for the first time. I didn't know what they were. I thought the mosquitoes were coming after us with torches.

I slept under the stars for the first time this summer. We didn't go camping; we had our roof repaired.

The food was so bad at summer camp. I threw my dinner in the river one night and the fish threw it back.

PUPIL: 'Teacher, it's the last day of school. This is the day I've been dreaming about for a long time.'
TEACHER: 'I know – you did a lot of that dreaming in class.'

'I just flew back from my holiday in Spain.'
'I bet your arms are tired.'

'I'm going to spend my holiday reviewing everything I learned at school.'
'Really? What are you going to do on the second day?'

What does the sun drink out of?

Sunglasses.

What do sheep do on sunny days?

Have a baa-baa-cue.

What do you call a cat at the beach?

Sandy Claws.

What do you call a snowman in July?

A puddle.

The seaside resort we visited last summer was so boring that one day the tide went out and never came back.

What did the beach say as the tide came in?

'Long time no sea.'

Where do cows go on their holidays?

Moo York.

Italy got Hungary ate Turkey slipped on Greece broke China went shopping in Iceland got eaten by Wales.

TEACHER: 'And what did you learn during the summer?'
PUPIL: 'I learned that three months is not enough time to tidy my room.'

I went to camp this summer and saw a lot of wild animals. In fact, several of them were my cabin mates.

Some of the kids got sick from the food at camp, but it was their own fault. They ate it.

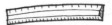

PUPIL: 'I plan to do absolutely nothing for the next three months.'
TEACHER: That should be easy. You've had nine months of practice doing that in school.'

'My teacher says that the summer holiday is not the time to stop learning.'
'I agree. I stopped learning way before the Christmas break.'

School Dinners

DINNER LADY: 'Eat up your greens, they are good for your skin.'
PUPIL: 'But I don't want green skin.'

63

How did the dinner lady get an electric shock?

She stepped on a bun and a current went up her leg.

TEACHER: 'Why are you the only one in class today?'
PUPIL: 'Because I missed school dinner yesterday.'

Where is the best place to have the sickroom at school?

Next to the canteen.

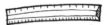

What do French pupils say after finishing their school dinners?

'Mercy.'

Why was the school soup rich?

Because it had twenty-four carrots in it.

What did the computer do at lunchtime?

Had a byte.

MOTHER: 'Why did you just swallow the money I gave you?'
SON: 'Well, you did say it was my lunch money.'

TEACHER: 'When do astronauts eat?'
PUPIL: 'At launch time.'

What kind of food do maths teachers eat?

Square meals.

The dinners at our school are so cold that even the potatoes wear their jackets.

PUPIL: 'Sir, are caterpillars good to eat?'
TEACHER: 'Of course not. Why do you ask?'
PUPIL: ''Cos you've just eaten one on your lettuce.'

What's the noisiest school dinner?

Bangers and mash.

PUPIL: 'There's a button in my soup.'
DINNER LADY: 'It must have fallen off when the salad was dressing.'

TEACHER: 'What do you suggest for a quick snack?'
DINNER LADY: 'Runner beans.'

What sits in custard looking cross?

Apple grumble.

I asked for gravy in the school canteen today and the dinner lady said, 'One lump or two?'

The food in our school canteen is so bad that teachers hand out second helpings as punishment.

I saw the recipe for the stew they serve in our school canteen. It begins: 'Take the ingredients from last week . . .'

If we ever study ancient history, the canteen will have the rolls to go with it.

FRED: 'How do they keep flies out of the kitchen in the school canteen?'
HARRY: 'They let them taste the food.'

FRED: 'Did you see the stew they served in the canteen today?'
HARRY: 'No, but I'll see it when they serve it again next week.'

I'll give you an idea how bad the food is in our school. When's the last time you saw hot dogs served with their tails between their legs?

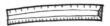

What's the best thing they've ever had in your school cafeteria?

A fire drill.

FRED: 'Excuse me, miss, but I'd like to know what's in today's stew.'
DINNER LADY: 'No, you wouldn't.'

FRED: 'Today's meal looks like spaghetti and meatballs.'
HARRY: 'Oh, good. For a minute there I thought it was shoelaces and hockey balls.'

We had a food fight in the school canteen today. The food won.

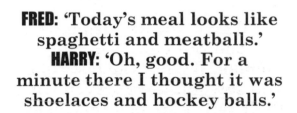

TEACHER: 'What started that food fight in the canteen?'
PUPIL: 'It started with the salad, then the meat loaf, and it ended with the dessert.'

MUM: 'From now on you're going to have free school dinners.'

SON: 'But, Mum, I don't want three school dinners, one is more than enough.'

DINNER LADY: 'It's very rude to reach over the table for cakes, haven't you got a tongue in your head?'

PUPIL: 'Yes, but my arms are longer.'

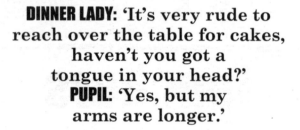

'Did you hear about the cruel school cook? She beats the eggs and whips the cream.'

Teachers

PUPIL: 'The art teacher doesn't like what I'm making.'
DAD: 'Why is that? What are you making?'
PUPIL: 'Mistakes.'

TEACHER: 'If you add 34,312 to 76,188, divide the answer by 3 and times by 4, what do you get?'
PUPIL: 'The wrong answer.'

MOTHER: 'How do you like your new teacher?'
SON: 'I don't. She told me to sit in the front row for the present and then she didn't give me one.'

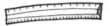

MOTHER: 'Does your teacher like you?'
SON: 'Like me? She loves me. Look at all those 'x's on my test paper.'

TEACHER: 'You aren't paying attention. Are you having trouble hearing?'
PUPIL: 'No, sir, I'm having trouble listening.'

Our teacher's a peach; she's got a heart of stone.

Our teacher's a treasure; we wonder where she was dug up.

Go to school to learn the three Rs: Ravage, Riot and Revolution

Teachers are very special; they're in a class of their own

Teacher is an anagram of cheater.

Our geography teacher is so bad he got lost showing some parents around the school.

'Our teacher talks to
herself; does yours?'
'Yes, but she doesn't realise
it; she thinks we're
actually listening.'

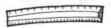

TEACHER: 'Why didn't you
answer me?'
PUPIL: 'I did; I shook my head.'
TEACHER: 'You don't expect
me to hear it rattling from
here, do you?'

TEACHER: 'I'd like to go through
one whole day without
having to tell you off.'
PUPIL: 'You have my
permission.'

TEACHER: 'Why were you late?'
PUPIL: 'Sorry, sir, I overslept.'
TEACHER: 'You mean you need to sleep at home too?'

TEACHER: 'You missed school yesterday, didn't you?'
PUPIL: 'Not very much.'

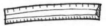

TEACHER: 'Fred, I told you to write this poem out ten times to improve your handwriting and you've only done it seven times?'
PUPIL: 'It seems that my counting isn't too good, either.'

79

TEACHER: 'I wish that you would pay a little attention.'
PUPIL: 'I'm paying as little as I can.'

TEACHER: 'What is the plural of mouse?'
PUPIL: 'Mice.'
TEACHER: 'Good, now what's the plural of baby?'
PUPIL: 'Twins.'

STUDENT: 'Sir, can I go to the bathroom?'
TEACHER: 'Not until you say your alphabet.'
STUDENT: 'A B C D E F G H I J K L M N O Q R S T U V W X Y and Z'
TEACHER: 'What happen to "P"?'
STUDENT: 'It's running down my leg.'

School Uniform

The dress code for members of staff at our school is simple: if you're not taken for one of the teachers, you're in trouble.

Our school has a strict dress code. The only time we can dress the way we like is on Halloween.

We have a very strict dress code at our school. Yesterday my lunch was punished because they said the brown paper bag it came in was offensive.

Our school has a simple rule as a dress code. If your parents wouldn't wear it, then you can't.

We have a kid in class
who dresses like a million
bucks. Everything he wears
is all wrinkled and green.

TEACHER: 'I think you have your
shoes on the wrong feet.'
PUPIL: 'No, I don't, miss. These
are the only feet I have.'

Classmates

One kid in our class is so dense he can't fill in his name on an application form unless it's a multiple choice question.

One of my classmates is
dangerously stupid.
He wanted to have his
address tattooed on the
inside of his eyelids so he
could find his way home
with his eyes closed.

A classmate of mine is so
smart, he knows the answer
to every question the teacher
asks. He raises his hand
so often in class that his
underarms are sunburned.

BULLY: 'Are you trying to make
a fool out of me?'
BOY: 'No, I never interfere
with nature.'

Two boys were fighting in the playground. The teacher separated them and said sternly, 'You mustn't behave like that. You must learn to give and take.'
'We did, miss,' replied one of the boys.
'He took my crisps and I gave him a thump.'

I had one friend who was a real dummy. He lost his shoes one time because he put them on the wrong feet. Then he couldn't remember whose feet he put them on.

I know one girl who has
to bring her parents to
school so often, they have
a better attendance
record than she has.

One friend of mine was
always being kept after
school. He spent so much
time at school, they
delivered his mail there.

Why did the school bully kick
the classroom computer?
Someone told him he
was supposed to boot
up the system.

School Rhymes

There was a headmaster from Quebec,
Who wrapped both his legs
round his neck,
But then he forgot,
How to untie the knot,
And now he's an absolute wreck.

There was a young teacher
from Harrow,
Whose nose was too long and
too narrow,
It gave so much trouble,
That he bent it up double,
And wheeled it around school
in a barrow.

There was a teacher called McGees,
Who thought he was going to sneeze.
The class said, 'Atchoo.'
McGees caught the flu,
And blew the class into the trees.

There was an old teacher
called Leach,
Who took the whole class
to the beach.
It said on a sign,
'Watch out for the mine,'
The last thing they heard was
his screech.

There once was a teacher from Leeds,
Who swallowed a packet of seeds.
In less than an hour,
Her nose was a flower,
And her hair was a bunch of weeds.

A teacher who looks like a bear,
Fell soundly asleep in his chair.
He woke with loud screaming,
Because he was dreaming,
His pupils had shaved off his hair.

There was a young teacher
called Emma,
Who was seized with a
terrible tremor.
She swallowed a spider.
Which wriggled inside her,
And left Emma in an
awful dilemma.

There was an old teacher
called Green,
Who invented a caning machine.
On the ninety ninth stroke,
The rotten thing broke,
And hit poor Green on the beam.

There was a
headmaster in Spain,
Who misguidedly prayed for rain.
The resultant showers,
Lasted for hours,
And washed his school
down the drain.

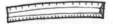

There was a young teacher
called Fisher,
Who was fishing for fish
in a fissure.
Then a seal, with a grin,
Pulled the teacher right in,
And now they're fishing the
fissure for Fisher.

No more pencils.
No more books.
No more teachers Dirty looks.

School is over.
School is done.
We can stop learning and
start having fun.

Readin', 'ritin', and 'rithmatic.
Nine months of that can
make you sick.
Readin', 'ritin', and history
Nine months of that's enough
for me.

What did I learn?
I don't remember.
And I'm not gonna try till
next September.